BEST SHOT

Written by Cathy Cassidy
Illustrated by Alan Brown

OXFORD
UNIVERSITY PRESS

Words to look out for ...

adapt (*verb*)
adapts, adapting, adapted
to change in order to cope with a new situation, or in order to get used to it

capable (*adjective*)
A capable person is able to do things well.

confidential (*adjective*)
Information is confidential when it has to be kept secret.

conform (*verb*)
conforms, conforming, conformed
To conform is to follow other people's rules or ideas about something.

distinguish (*verb*)
distinguishes, distinguishing, distinguished
To distinguish between things is to notice or show the differences between them.

examine (*verb*)
examines, examining, examined
To examine something is to look at it closely or in detail.

improvise (*verb*)
improvises, improvising, improvised
To improvise is to perform something by making it up as you go along, rather than saying, singing or playing what is written down.

interior (*noun*)
the inside of something

refer (*verb*)
refers, referring, referred
To refer to someone or something is to mention them or speak about them.

resolve (*verb*)
resolves, resolving, resolved
To resolve to do something is to decide to do it.

Introducing ...

DINO
(story narrator)

ABE
(Dino's best friend)

SYLVIE
(Dino's mum)

CAROLE
(Abe's mum)

STEFANO
(Melody's dad and Sylvie's boyfriend)

MELODY
(Stefano's daughter)

NINA
(a girl in Dino's class)

Chapter 1

I'm standing at the end of the pier in Thornton-on-Sea, looking out across the glittering water.

'What's up, Dino?' my best friend Abe wants to know. 'Seen a whale or something?'

'Nah,' I tell him. 'Just ... looking. If you look hard enough, you can see forever!'

'What d'you mean?' Abe asks. 'Forever isn't a place!'

I grin. 'I know, right? It's just something my dad used to say. Load of rubbish, huh?'

It didn't feel like rubbish when Dad first said it, though. Whenever I'm on the pier, I can't help trying to see forever. It's no use. I can't even see Brighton, just along the coast, and definitely not New Zealand, where Dad lives now. I have no chance of seeing forever and none of seeing Dad anytime soon either.

When Mum and Dad divorced, they promised that nothing would change. They

said I'd still see Dad as much as before. That was rubbish too, because then he got offered a job in New Zealand and left Thornton-on-Sea before I could blink.

There's no such thing as forever. I know that better than most.

I push all thoughts of Dad away and lift up my phone. Mum finally let me have one so I could stay in touch with Dad, but it's great for filming too.

'Action!' I call to Abe, pressing the record button. His model rocket glides smoothly into view. I follow it across the water. You can hardly see the fishing line it dangles from.

Once I get some special effects sorted, this video will look awesome.

'Cut!' I say. Abe lowers the fishing rod, complete with swinging rocket. 'Nobody will ever know it's made from cardboard and tinfoil!'

'This could be our best film yet,' replies Abe. 'I've almost finished the alien puppets. They're properly scary!'

Abe is fantastic at making models. I'm pretty good at making up stories and stuff. We make a great team, and I'm not just saying that.

'Ready to go back?' I check. 'I told Mum we'd only be ten minutes. If we get them in a good mood, they might let us have ice cream.'

We race along the pier towards the Beach Cafe. I can see Mum through the window, drinking tea and talking to Abe's mum, Carole, who works there. Carole is pretending to wipe the table, but really she's chatting to my mum.

Abe lives next door to me. Our mums are best mates. They never seem to run out of things to talk about, and today it looks like they're sharing an especially juicy secret.

'Ice cream, boys?' Mum asks, as we walk in. She waves some money at me. 'Let us finish our chat in peace.'

Abe and I go to order. I buy two cones with strawberry sauce. Back at the next table, I hear a bit of their confidential chat.

Information is confidential when it has to be kept secret.

Mum's talking about her upcoming birthday treat, a night away with her new boyfriend. She's been seeing Stefano for eight months now. Although I've met him a few times, I am not a fan.

Mum says he was married to someone famous, but he acts like *he's* the famous one. He tries to be nice, but I already have a dad, even if he is thousands of miles away.

Stefano met Mum at the comedy club where she sometimes does a stand-up show. She actually works at a care home, but since the divorce she's 'reinvented herself' as a comedian. It's the most embarrassing thing ever. I've seen her rehearsing and half her material is based on me! I mean, cheers, Mum ... not.

Anyway, Stefano thought Mum's act was so great, he offered to be her manager. Soon after that he asked her out, so now he's her boyfriend, too. Stefano buys Mum fancy meals and flowers. I just don't like him.

We always used to get a takeaway and watch TV on our birthdays. Now, all of a sudden, birthdays have gone posh. Stefano is taking her for a night away at some swish hotel. Mum's had her hair done specially and bought a new dress. Yuck, right?

'I'm going to be late for work,' Mum says to Carole, grabbing her bag. 'And you need to close up. I'll keep you posted ... Thanks for agreeing to have Dino tomorrow night.'

'No trouble at all,' Carole says. 'Abe loves having him stay over.'

'Come on, Dino,' Mum says.

I wave goodbye to Abe, hurrying after her. We make it to the care home with minutes to spare. Mum's boss lets me come with her on afternoon and evening shifts since Dad left. Actually, I really like it here.

Sometimes I do my homework. Sometimes I chat to Stan about when he was a postman, or to Edie about being a scientist. Most of the residents have stories to tell.

Tonight, I need to do my maths homework. One of the new residents, Shona, used to work as a teacher at a tiny school in the Scottish Highlands. She gives me a hand, but I find it hard to concentrate.

Mum's birthday and Stefano's stupid hotel treat keep sneaking into my mind. I don't know why the thought bugs me so much. I should be happy that Stefano's making a fuss of Mum, but I'm not. Things are changing – and I don't like that at all.

Chapter 2

Friendships seem to get more complicated the older you get. It used to be just kicking a ball around the playground. Year 6 is different: it's like there are all these new rules that nobody tells you about.

Nina Reddy used to play football with us. Sometimes she even shared a chocolate bar with me and we'd talk about old sci-fi movies because she and her dad liked them. Now, she swans around like she's royalty, a gaggle of admirers in her wake. Nina knows all the unspoken rules about how to be cool. She has become the most popular girl in the class. These days she doesn't share her chocolate with me or talk about sci-fi.

Abe and I are neither cool nor popular. We don't conform. We're just ... us.

Abe talks too much about things the cool kids label 'boring', like making models,

---

To conform is to follow other people's rules or ideas about something.

or whether there could be aliens living under the school kitchen, or if Ms Kowalski the headteacher is secretly part werewolf. (She isn't, but Abe has a very active imagination.) Sometimes I see Nina and her crew roll their eyes at Abe. If I were brave, I'd stick up for him, but mostly I stay quiet and get on with my work.

Today our teacher, Mr Murray, announces that we'll be putting on a school play before the spring holidays.

'There are nice parts for those of you who

like drama. It's a musical, so there are great songs, too,' he says. 'There will be something for everyone: either performing or behind the scenes. Auditions are next Friday.'

Half the hands in the class shoot up.

Nina just smiles, quietly confident.

'You'll get a lead role, Nina,' one of her friends whispers. 'No contest!'

Abe and I exchange glances. There's no way we'll bother with the auditions. There might be some behind-the-scenes stuff we could do, like scenery painting or prop making ... that'd be much more our thing.

Finally it's 3pm and we're let out into the sunny afternoon air.

'Think we could get Mr Murray to do a sci-fi play?' Abe is asking. 'Like a Martian invasion musical or something entirely set on a spaceship?'

'Nah, sounds like he's got something in mind already,' I say. 'But we can start editing our space rocket film after dinner instead ...'

'Mum says we should make cookies for your mum's birthday,' Abe says.

I grin. 'Great! I'll have to call Dad, too. We always video call on Fridays.'

We stop to buy chocolate chips on the way home. It's only February but the supermarket has small bunches of daffodils. Yellow is Mum's favourite colour, so I use some pocket money to buy a bunch.

We break into a run towards Abe's terraced house, laughing. I stick the flowers in a jar of water to stay fresh until Mum's home tomorrow. We eat beans on toast for dinner, then tie on aprons. Abe's mum has set out a mixing bowl and the ingredients for cookies.

'Chocolate chip is the best kind of cookie,'

Abe comments as he sifts the flour.

I scan the recipe. 'It makes loads!' I say.

'Tomorrow's your Mum's birthday,' Abe's mum points out. 'You might have … visitors.'

'Nah,' I say, stirring the mixture while Abe helps himself to chocolate chips. 'We'll probably just watch TV. Tonight is Mum's special night away with Stefano. Tomorrow things will be back to normal.'

Abe's mum frowns. 'Hmm. I thought Stefano and Melody might …'

'Melody?' I say quickly.

'You know,' she says smiling brightly. 'Melody … Stefano's daughter!'

I remember being told that Stefano had a daughter, but I've never actually met her.

'She definitely won't be coming over, and nor will Stefano,' I say. 'No, it'll just be me and Mum and all these cookies. And I'm not complaining!'

I dollop the last few spoonfuls of mixture onto a baking tray.

'OK if we go out to the den?' Abe asks. 'To continue working on the film we're making?'

'Of course! I'll make you hot chocolates as a special treat.'

By the time the hot chocolate is made, the cookies are out of the oven. They sit cooling on a rack, smelling awesome. Mum's going to love them!

We go out the back door and hop over the fence to the den in my back yard. It's actually the old garage that goes with our house. We don't have a car, so Dad turned it into a den for Abe and me years ago. The interior is papered with old sci-fi movie pictures and there are two old armchairs, too.

When I started getting into making films,

The interior means the inside of something.

Dad gave me his old laptop. He showed me how to do some amazing special effects. I'm pretty good at it now. I work on the space rocket video, playing with the colours and adding a voiceover.

Abe works on his alien puppets. 'Y'know, we should start putting our videos online,' he suggests. 'If our mums let us. We'd get loads of likes!'

'Maybe,' I say. 'I'll think about it.' I'm not sure it's a great idea, though. I don't think the films are good enough yet. Besides, there's more to life than 'likes'.

When my phone rings, I've almost forgotten about my video call with Dad.

'Hey, Dad!' I say. 'I'm in the den with Abe, working on a new film.'

I can't help feeling sad because he's so far away and because Mum is having a special night away with Stefano.

'Excellent,' Dad says. 'How's it going? Is my old computer software still OK?'

'Yeah, great!' I tell him. 'Our new film is about aliens taking over Thornton-on-Sea ...'

'Love it!' he says. 'How's school?'

'They're putting on a play. Abe and I might help out behind the scenes.'

Dad grins. 'Great! Dino, you've remembered it's your mum's birthday tomorrow, haven't you?'

'I bought some flowers and baked cookies with Abe,' I say. 'I haven't forgotten!'

'OK, mate, sounds good. Wish her all the best from me!'

'I will.'

Later that night, I roll over in my sleeping bag. I'm on the blow-up mattress in Abe's room. I've made a card, put the cookies in a tin, checked the flowers still look good ... Tomorrow I will wish Mum the best from Dad, even though I think it's rubbish that he's miles away. He should be here with us, where he belongs.

I pull the sleeping bag up and drift into sleep.

Chapter 3

Mum comes in just as Abe and I are munching our cereal. She looks different somehow. She's wearing a new silky top and glittery make-up. She must have had a good time, because she's glowing with happiness. If you plugged her in, the energy she's giving out could power Thornton-on-Sea for a week.

'Dino!' she beams, grabbing me in a hug.

'Mum, gerroff!' I say, pulling free. 'Happy Birthday! I bought flowers and made you cookies. Abe helped too.'

'How lovely! Thank you, boys!' she says. 'And it *is* a happy birthday, too …'

She does a dramatic pose, hands framing her face. 'I'm so happy!'

Abe's mum grins, and even Abe digs me in the ribs. I look at them, confused. What is going on?

Mum is gushing. 'Carole, I'll tell you all about it later. But … it was just perfect! I can't quite believe it!'

Mum is making no sense at all. 'Believe what?' I ask.

She doesn't answer but says instead, 'C'mon, let's get you home. Get the place tidy for later.'

At home, a bunch of flowers as big as me is sitting on the table. From Stefano, for sure. I stick my drooping daffodils on the windowsill and arrange the cookies on a plate.

Mum's smile is about a mile wide. She's spraying furniture polish everywhere, even though the house is already tidy. 'Will you

help me pop new bedding on the spare bed?' she asks.

'Why, are we expecting someone?'

'I'll explain in a minute,' she says. She shakes a pink sheet from its wrapping. 'Let's just get everything straight.'

Once the bedding is on, Mum arranges a couple of fluffy cushions on top.

'There,' she says. 'That's better!'

'Mum,' I say. 'What's going on? Why are you acting so ... strange?'

Mum smiles. 'Oh, Dino, I don't know how to say this. Last night ... it was really wonderful. The hotel, the dinner, the music ...'

'Hmm,' I mumble.

'It was so romantic,' Mum explains. 'And Stefano ... well. You know we've been seeing a lot of each other? Dino, we've decided to make a go of it!'

I blink. 'A go of what?'

'Life,' Mum says. 'Dino, he's asked me to marry him!'

She holds out her left hand. Suddenly I see what Abe and his mum spotted earlier. It should have been obvious all along.

A diamond engagement ring on Mum's finger. My legs turn to jelly. I have to sit down on the bed before I fall.

'You're getting married?' I whisper. 'But ... why?'

'He's a good man, Dino,' Mum says gently. 'We love each other. And of course, with Stefano comes Melody ...'

Melody. Stefano's daughter. The new bedding, the fluffy cushions ... they must be for her. Cold panic floods through me.

'Tell me they're not coming here,' I say. 'To our house? To stay the night?'

Mum bites her lip. 'It'll be for a lot longer than that,' she says.

My eyes open wide. 'They're moving in? I've never even *met* Melody!'

'That's my fault,' Mum says. 'I didn't realize

things would move this fast, but Stefano's right. You have to grab happiness when you find it. You'll like Melody. She's a lovely girl, nearly eleven, bright and lively and into making videos, just like you.'

'When are they coming?' I demand, my voice gruff.

She checks her phone. 'Quite soon, actually,' she says. 'No point delaying things once a decision is made, is there?'

As if on cue, the doorbell chimes, and I look out of the window to see Stefano unloading suitcases from a shiny car. A tall girl with long hair and dark eyes stands on the pavement beside him, surveying the street with horror.

Mum gallops downstairs and throws the door wide, ushering them inside. There's lots of hugging from Stefano and lots of scowling from Melody.

'Dino!' Stefano booms. I'm perched gloomily on the stairs.

'Looks like we'll be getting to know each other a whole lot better now,' he says. 'Melody, meet Dino! You're nearly the same age, so you'll be in the same class. Won't that be fun?'

About as much fun as my dad moving away, I think. Melody seems as stunned at this whole situation as I am.

'Is this it?' she asks, as she looks around our little living room. 'Seriously?'

Mum keeps smiling. 'It's smaller than you're used to,' she says. 'But once you unpack, it'll feel more like home.'

'I don't think so,' Melody says.

Ditching her suitcases, Melody pushes past me and stomps up the stairs. She finds her room and slams the door so hard it makes the walls shake.

Stefano's smile fades.

'She's not happy right now, Dino, but she'll soon settle,' he says. 'Give her time.' He turns to Mum.

'Sylvie, it's still your birthday … sit down. Put your feet up! Let's all celebrate!'

My Mum is planning to marry this random man with a drama queen daughter, and they want me to celebrate? No chance.

Chapter 4

I was devastated when Mum and Dad split up, even though they both insisted it was for the best. I was devastated when Dad moved to New Zealand, too. Right now, though, he's the only one I want to talk to.

I make an unplanned video call to Dad the next morning.

'You're kidding, mate!' he says. 'Engaged? Wow. That's a lot for you to take in, Dino.'

'You didn't know?' I check. 'I think Carole next door did. Maybe Abe knew, too?' I remember his dig in the ribs when he spotted Mum's engagement ring.

'I didn't know,' Dad promises. 'I saw it coming, though, from the way your mum's been talking about Stefano. And they've moved in? Stefano and Melody?'

Dad saw it coming? I know he talks to Mum sometimes, but how come he saw it coming and I didn't?

'Yeah, they have,' I whisper. I keep half an eye on the bedroom door in case Melody's outside listening. 'Melody's terrible, Dad. She thinks she's so much better than everyone else. She hates it here!'

'This must be tough for her too,' Dad points out. 'From what your mum's said, Melody's had a lot to cope with. Losing her mother so young. Losing that whole celebrity lifestyle ...'

I frown. 'I don't know anything about that.'

'Maybe ask her,' Dad suggests. 'I know this is sudden, but it could be a good thing if it makes your mum happy. Things change ... you have to adapt to the situation!'

'I don't want to adapt to anything,' I huff.

To adapt to a new situation is to change in order to cope with it, or in order to get used to it.

'Give Melody a chance,' Dad says. 'She's on your territory. Just try and make her feel welcome.'

This is not what I wanted to hear, not at all.

Still, a part of me is glad to see Mum smiling again. I guess Dad's right ... I have to make the best of this. I resolve to at least *try* to make friends with Melody.

I find her in the kitchen, peering crossly at the cornflakes. She's wearing leggings and a posh-looking jumper. She looks out of place amongst the jumble of dinner plates, stacked ready for washing up.

'I usually have a croissant for breakfast,'

To resolve to do something is to decide to do it.

Melody grumbles. 'I don't suppose there are any?'

'I don't even know what one is,' I admit.

'A French pastry, sort of flaky and … oh, never mind!'

She shakes cereal into a bowl. 'You probably don't get them in this dump. This will have to do.'

I sigh. 'Look, Melody, I know you're not happy about this. I'm not either, but Mum and your dad are. We'll have to give it our best shot, right? Adapt to this new situation. Thornton-on-Sea isn't a dump, honestly. It's great!'

Melody rolls her eyes. 'You have *no* idea,' she says. 'We lived in London before. We had this big flat overlooking the river. We used to go on holiday to Milan and New York. I went to a private school. So yes, actually, this place *is* a dump. It really is.'

'Right,' I mutter, but then stop.

A tear slides slowly down Melody's cheek

To adapt to a new situation is to change in order to cope with it, or in order to get used to it.

and drops into the cornflakes.

It's kind of shocking. I hand her a tissue from the box on the table. She wipes her eyes furiously.

'It'll be OK,' I say, although I have no idea whether it will be.

Melody laughs, but it's a sad, hollow sound. 'It all went wrong when Mum died,' she tells me. 'You've heard of her, obviously ... Melanie Morris. She was runner-up on that *Housemates* reality TV show, before I was born. She was famous. TV shows and magazines couldn't get enough of her. Dad was her manager. When I came along, I was famous, too. I still am, really.'

'Sounds ... great,' I say, just to be polite. I have zero interest in reality TV, but I don't want to be rude.

'Mum died two years ago,' Melody says. My jaw drops open. 'She was ill. It was all over the newspapers. You probably heard.'

'Probably,' I say, although I'm pretty sure I didn't. 'I'm really sorry, Melody.'

'You and me both, Dino. Dad had to sell our home. Now we're here. Dad isn't making much money these days. No more flashy holidays. No more private school. And now he's fallen for Sylvie. I mean, your mum is OK, but she'll never replace my mum!'

'Course not,' I say. 'Stefano will never replace my dad, either.'

Melody sighs. 'Dad's got this idea that I need a regular "small-town childhood". He says that all I think about is being famous, and that it's not good for me. I have my own online channel, you see – Melody Morris.'

'I'm an influencer, a rising star,' Melody continues. 'Mum helped me get started when I was seven. It's built up from there ...'

I try to get my head around this. 'An influencer?' I echo.

Melody pulls a face. 'Dad said you make videos. I thought you'd at least be into this kind of stuff!' She takes out her mobile and clicks a couple of times. A video of her wearing a hat with fake animal ears pops up. I listen as she chats to the camera about how amazing the hat is.

'Companies send me stuff for free,' she tells me, 'and I have to pretend I love it. I've got loads of followers and get tons of likes ...'

'For saying you like things you don't?'

Melody shrugs. 'I don't like Thornton-on-Sea,' she says. 'It's so ... ordinary. I'm just not cut out for ordinary!' she continues.

'I'll show you my favourite places,' I suggest. 'Prove to you it's not so ordinary, if you like?'

'Maybe,' she says, sulkily.

'Thornton-on-Sea's great,' I tell her. 'It's not exactly Hollywood, but who needs all that anyway? Pretend you like it. Rise above the ordinary!'

Melody frowns. 'So what you're saying is ... there's a bit of sparkle everywhere. Even in Thornton-on-Sea!'

I wasn't saying that, exactly, but I nod anyway. 'Sure,' I say. 'Whatever.'

Melody grins, and her whole face lights up. 'Rise above the ordinary,' she says. 'I like it! That's not such a bad idea, Dino. Find the sparkle! Yes! I'll get started straight away!'

She sweeps out of the kitchen like a small whirlwind.

Chapter 5

'Did you know about all this?' I ask Abe the next morning. We usually walk to school together, so he always comes to mine first thing. 'Because if you knew, why didn't you say? We're supposed to be friends.'

Abe's face clouds. 'I didn't know,' he says. 'Honest! At least, not exactly. Mum kept dropping hints that something was going on, but I didn't actually think …'

Hurt fizzes up inside me. 'No, you didn't think at all,' I snap.

I know none of this is Abe's fault. All the same, I had to wait half an hour for Melody to get out of the bathroom this morning. Now I feel all spiky and mean.

'I'm not walking in today,' I tell him. 'Stefano's driving us.'

'Oh, and I can't work on the film this week,' I add. 'I don't have time for cardboard space rockets right now.'

I see the shock on Abe's face as I slam the front door. It doesn't make me feel any better. If anything, it makes me feel worse.

Later, sitting alone at the back of the class, I watch Melody stroll into the classroom. It's like she owns the place. Mr Murray introduces her. Melody scans the room, taking it all in. When she spots Nina she grins, a bright, starry kind of grin. It's as if she's recognized one of her own.

By lunchtime the two of them are like best friends. I watch them in the dinner hall as they laugh and chat.

They bond over plans to audition for the school play. They chat about Melody's video channel, and they discuss her famous mum.

There's no sign of the moody, tearful Melody I saw yesterday. Or the one that hogged the bathroom this morning and then left wet towels on the floor. This version of Melody has charm by the sackful, and the cool kids are eating out of her hand.

'I've had this brilliant idea for my channel,' she tells Nina. 'All about moving to Thornton-on-Sea and finding sparkle in unexpected places. I thought I'd call it "Rise Above the Ordinary!"'

I catch Melody's eye and raise an eyebrow. She pretends not to notice, just like she's pretending that this is her idea, not mine.

'You can all be in it!' she's saying.

Then her phone is out, and I start to panic because clearly nobody has explained that our school has a no-mobiles-in-school rule. She starts filming a little clip of Nina eating

salad and quiche. Melody will get in trouble if she goes on like this, but Nina and her friends seem to be loving the rule breaking.

I spot Abe at the edge of the hall. He's clearly unsure if he should join me, but I'm not ready to forgive him yet. I take my tray and head to the clearing trolley.

'Dino!' Melody calls, waving wildly. 'Hey, new step-bro, come and sit with us!'

I stop, startled, then sit down awkwardly opposite Melody. Nina smiles brightly, as if she's seeing me for the first time since Year 3.

'So, you know I mentioned my dad was a promoter?' Melody is telling her new friends.

'He's just started managing Dino's mum, who's an amazing stand-up comedian!' Melody continues.

'She's going to be famous! And Dino's a film-maker, too, a bit like me ...'

'Your mum's a comedian?' Nina asks. 'That's so cool!'

'Suppose so,' I mumble. I'm shocked that Melody's told my classmates about Mum. I'm also a bit excited to be sitting with the cool kids – Nina, Kiran, Tash and Jojo don't normally notice I'm alive. I see Abe watching from the back of the hall.

'OK, Dino ... record us!' Melody commands.

'I can't,' I tell her. 'There are no phones allowed in school!'

'Don't be so boring!' Melody scoffs. 'I'm an influencer, remember? Oh, forget it. I'll do it!'

She turns her phone to selfie mode and throws an arm around Nina's shoulders.

'Hi, everyone! This is Melody with a quick post to keep you up to speed! Here I am on

my very first day at Thornton-on-Sea Primary. This is my new friend, Nina! Say hello, Nina!'

Nina waves at the camera. 'I'm going to improvise here. What you need to know is that this is an ordinary school in an ordinary town. But my new friends are EXTRA-ordinary! I'm here to tell you we can all rise above the ordinary! We can find the sparkle wherever we are. I'll be back soon with lots of cool life tips. Not to mention great new products and, of course, my new best friends! Bye for now!'

Nina's friends crowd into the frame, waving and laughing.

To improvise is to perform something by making it up as you go along, rather than saying, singing or playing what is written down.

Melody waves at the camera and clicks to end the video.

'You really shouldn't be filming in school like that,' I say again.

'I've not been caught yet, have I, Dino?' Melody says. 'Chill out, step-bro! So, we're all trying out for the school play? That's exciting! Obviously, I'm going for the lead role …'

'Me too,' Nina chips in. 'The auditions are on Friday.'

'They are,' Melody says, and although her smile is bright, her eyes look flinty. 'May the best girl win!'

Melody has certainly made a big impression on her first day.

Later on, in the den, I show her how to add some fancy filters and special effects to her video. She squeals all over again, delighted.

'This is going to put my channel right up there! I'll be a top influencer,' Melody says. 'Thanks, Dino!'

'It's OK,' I say.

'With your tech skills and my talent, I can take this to the next level,' she declares. 'Just wait till I land the main role in the play ... I'll ask if you can film it. If I post some clips online, I might get spotted for a big West End show! It could be my big break!'

'Er ... not sure we'd be allowed to do that,' I mutter.

'Of course we will. And I can talk about all kinds of stuff. Important stuff. Advising people how to live their best life!'

'But ... aren't you a bit young for that?'

'So?' Melody says. 'I can still be a lifestyle expert. The youngest one ever, maybe!'

'I can talk about friendship,' she says, 'and starting a new school. And what it's like to suddenly have a new family. We can do a video of the wedding, right? I want a big flouncy bridesmaid's dress and everything!'

Mum has been clear that there will be no flouncy dresses. It will be small and simple. The registry office is booked and there's talk of a private party in the Beach Cafe. Melody seems to want something far swankier.

'What sort of films do you make?' Melody asks.

'All sorts really,' I reply. 'I'd like to get into documentaries. Do something at the care home where Mum works. Maybe record some of the residents' stories. They've had amazing lives!'

Melody wrinkles her nose, which tells me exactly what she thinks of that idea.

She pauses to look around the den. She takes in the tatty armchairs and the editing desk. Her gaze falls on Abe's table. It's strewn

with modelling clay, paints, brushes, glue, cardboard, tinfoil and more.

'What is all this?' she asks, examining a half-made puppet. 'It's like a toddler's craft club! They're not yours, are they?'

I frown. I love Abe's models and his creative ideas for the films we make together. However, looking at them through Melody's eyes, I can see they must look silly.

'No, not mine,' I say. 'Abe makes them, for the films we do. Used to do. I've sort of outgrown them.'

'I can imagine,' she says.

I don't argue. After all, I seem to be in with the cool kids now.

To examine something is to look at it closely or in detail.

Chapter 6

As I'm not filming with Abe, I suddenly have lots of free time. I resolve to take Melody around my favourite places in Thornton-on-Sea. It's cold and grey, but I film Melody on the pier, the beach, and outside the cafe for her 'Rise Above the Ordinary' channel. Then she grabs the phone and films a boarded-up shop with a broken window. An overflowing litter bin and a broken umbrella get the same treatment.

Suddenly there's a downpour, so we run home before we get drenched. I'm not sure I've convinced Melody this place is cool yet.

But I am getting used to waiting for her to finish in the bathroom. I am even getting used to hearing her practise her song, ready for tomorrow's audition.

To resolve to do something is to decide to do it.

I'm no expert, but it doesn't seem to be going well.

'Test me on my lines?' she asks.

The first read-through is so wooden it's painful. Melody sounds like she's reading from a shopping list. It's so different from her videos.

'I think you need to do it with a bit more emotion,' I tell her.

So the next time she wipes imaginary tears from her eyes. It's even worse than the shopping list version. Melody can't seem to distinguish between reading with feeling and totally overdoing it. It's bad, and I think she knows it.

'I'm better than Nina,' she insists. 'Nina can sing, sure. But I was in a TV ad for washing powder when I was three! With my mum! I have star quality. Real stage presence. Am I right?'

To distinguish between things is to notice or show the differences between them.

'Possibly,' I say.

This clearly isn't the right answer. Melody spirals off into a terrifying rant.

'Nobody here knows talent when they see it! All that filming today?' she snarls. 'Maybe I'll put the clips together. Make something that tells the truth about this dump of a place. Including the boring people in it!'

She stomps upstairs and slams the door.

I'm starting to see that my new stepsister is a kind of human storm cloud. I'm dreading tomorrow. If Melody doesn't get that part, there will be trouble. BIG trouble.

On top of all this, I'm really missing Abe. He's not stressful to be around. Making films about space rockets and aliens was way more interesting than filming Melody going on about the true meaning of friendship.

I don't think she has a clue about that. I'm not sure I do either, taking my anger out on Abe like that. I tried to talk to him after school today, but he just walked away.

We all head to the hall on Friday morning, even those of us who aren't auditioning. I doodle film ideas in my notebook and only properly look up when Nina starts to sing. She's really good.

Then I watch Melody's audition. It's truly terrible. Her confidence seems to have melted away, and she looks sick with nerves. She forgets some of the song lyrics and starts singing random stuff instead. Some of the other kids laugh. Her acting attempt isn't much better. It's painful to watch.

How can someone so cool and comfortable with cameras freeze and panic when asked to sing or act? I'm pretty sure Melody's as shocked as I am. We head back to class. Melody's looking really upset.

At lunchtime, it all blows up. We're eating together when Mr Murray comes in and pins up the cast list. A bunch of kids race to check it out.

It's no surprise Nina got the starring role. Melody? She's only in the chorus. A background performer.

Ouch.

'She might be called Melody, but she can't hold a tune,' someone mutters. Melody must have heard because her face turns scarlet.

'You must be joking!' she rages. 'Sorry, Nina. You've got an OK singing voice, it's true. But you do NOT have star quality. At all. Mr Murray probably felt sorry for you ...'

'Melody, don't,' I tug at her sleeve. 'Leave it!'

But Melody can't leave it. She starts

referring to all the reasons why Nina is wrong for the part. Nina just tilts her head to one side and listens. Finally, when Melody runs out of steam, Nina speaks.

'I think your mum was pretty cool,' she says. 'I thought you might be, too, Melody, but you're not. You're mean, jealous, spiteful … and fake!'

Then Nina turns and walks away, her friends following.

Just when I think it can't get any worse, the headteacher, Ms Kowalski, strides into the hall. She has a face like thunder.

'Melody Morris, come to my office now!' she barks.

The last wisps of confidence fall away from my soon-to-be stepsister. She looks confused and shocked.

She follows Ms Kowalski out of the dining hall.

To refer to someone or something is to mention them or speak about them.

That's the last I see of her until later. When I glance out of the classroom window, I spot Stefano marching her out of school. This looks serious. It can't just be because of the row with Nina, surely?

Back at home, Melody is in her room in disgrace. 'What happened?' I ask Stefano. 'What did she do?'

He shakes his head. 'What didn't she do? Melody made a video saying Thornton-on-Sea is a dump. She described her new friends as boring and talentless. Someone saw it and called your headteacher. Understandably, Ms Kowalski is furious. With me. With Melody. With social media in general.'

'Yikes,' I say.

'Yikes indeed,' Stefano says. 'And that's not all. Melody didn't think the no-mobiles rule applied to her. She filmed her classmates and posted the videos online. It's terrible!'

'That's not good,' I say.

'I've taken down Melody's channel,' Stefano

goes on. 'She says she made the video when she was upset. She was stressed before the auditions. Apparently, she never meant for anybody to see it. Looks like she accidentally made it live, though, and it's upset some people. I blame myself ... I should have been checking her content much more. Melody knew what the boundaries were, but she decided to ignore them. I've been too distracted recently to notice. It's my fault.'

Stefano is right about that. Allowing a ten-year-old drama queen so much freedom was definitely asking for trouble.

He sighs. 'This is a wake-up call for me and Melody, both. Things are going to change. Not the best start to life here, Dino, is it?'

'No,' I say. 'Not the best.'

Not even a week here, and Melody has completely destroyed her channel. So much for 'Rise Above the Ordinary'.

So much for posts about friendship and finding the sparkle. Right now, Melody doesn't have a friend to her name. Actually, I'm not sure I do either.

I fish the last cookies from the tin and knock on Melody's door.

'Go away!' she growls.

'Can I come in?' I persist.

I hear her blowing her nose, followed by a muffled, 'Suppose so ...'

I push open the door and go in. Melody is wrapped in a fleece blanket, eyes damp from crying. She glares at me. 'Come to tell me I'm mean, jealous and spiteful?' she asks. 'I know that already. Come to tell me I know nothing about friendship? Guess what? I know that, too!'

'I didn't see what you posted,' I say. 'I don't think any of the kids at school did ...'

'I hope not. I meant to set it to private!' she wails.

'I'd never have said those things if I'd thought ... well, I suppose I never should have said them in the first place. I did it yesterday. I was angry. I knew I'd struggle with that audition. I wanted it so much, Dino! Now I'll have to watch Nina swanning around, getting all the star treatment.'

'Nina's OK,' I say gently. 'She'll be brilliant in the play. C'mon, Melody. Who needs the star treatment, anyway?'

She sniffs. 'I do, Dino,' she says. 'It's all I know. I'm good in front of a camera. Just not so good at actual acting. Or singing, clearly!

'And now Dad's taken my channel down. He's going to triple-check every single thing I do in future. He was supposed to anyway, but I took advantage while he's been so distracted with your mum. Ms Kowalski is furious – I've been banned from performing in the play altogether!'

'That's harsh,' I say, although I think it's actually pretty fair. Melody broke the rules, so she's got to pay the penalty.

'I've really messed up!' Melody wails. 'No channel, no friends, no school play. How did I get everything so wrong?'

'It's a skill,' I tease. Melody smiles, just a little. 'We could make a film together,' I suggest. 'You might not be an actress, but you are good in front of a camera. A natural, really! We could do a documentary, maybe? Instead of telling people what *you* think, you could ask them what *they* think?'

A plan is unfolding in my mind, one that could work for both of us. 'We'll work something out soon,' I tell her. 'Right now, there's someone I want to talk to about friendship.'

I go downstairs, step over the wall and knock on Abe's door.

Chapter 7

Abe doesn't exactly look pleased to see me.

'What do you want, Dino?'

'To say sorry,' I tell him. 'I was mean and selfish. I took my temper out on you. I really am sorry.'

Abe shrugs. 'Yeah? Are you sure about that? Or did you just lose your cool-kid mates and need someone to talk to?'

'I don't care about the cool kids,' I say. 'I miss you, Abe. I miss making our sci-fi films and thinking up script ideas. I miss hanging out in the den together. I miss making hot chocolate and dunking our biscuits in it. I messed up, but I want to put it right. You're my best friend!'

'So ... how will you put it right?'

I grin. 'I'll be goalie every time we play footy!' He smiles a bit so I carry on. 'I'll write a new script about the aliens who live beneath the school kitchen ... ' He smiles again.

'I'll give you my aubergine curry every time it's on the school dinner menu ...'

'Yeah? How about when they have baked potato with cheesy beans?'

'You're pushing it now,' I say, laughing. 'Are we OK, then?'

'We're OK,' Abe says. 'I suppose.'

I breathe a huge sigh of relief. 'Come over to the den,' I say. 'I've had an idea for a different sort of film. A documentary. I need someone to help with props and lighting and stuff, if you're up for it?'

'I'll think about it,' Abe says, grinning.

A week later, I'm at the care home, setting up the camera. Abe is messing about with lamps. Melody scans the questions on her clipboard. She looks less starry than usual

in a knitted jumper and her hair in bunches.

We're here to interview a woman called Marie. We'll ask what it was like growing up in Jamaica. Next week we're talking to Stan about his days as a country postman. Mum says our interviews are a great way to record the residents' memories. The care home boss approves and Stefano is finally happy. He says that if things turn out well then maybe, just maybe, we could put something in for a film competition he's heard about.

'Maybe I can share it on my channel?' Melody asks now.

'This isn't about you, Melody,' Mum reminds her. 'You're doing this because it's a wonderful thing to do. You guys want to be taken seriously, don't you?'

'Definitely,' Abe and I chorus.

Melody pouts. 'I'll take that as a 'no' then. Oh well! I'll give it my best shot.' She guides Marie over to where we've set up the lights.

The filming goes brilliantly. Melody asks

great questions and listens carefully. She's warm, capable and confident. She makes Marie feel like her story is the most fascinating thing she's ever heard. I love the bit about how six-year-old Marie was amazed to see her first ever snow start to fall as she walked off the ship onto British soil. When the interview's over, Melody leans over to give Marie a hug.

She didn't get a part in the school play, but I can totally see Melody having her own chat show one day.

'How cool was that?' she says as we pack everything up. 'Better than waffling on about animal hats and fluffy toys. Marie's had an amazing life. I helped her tell that story. Well, we all did!'

'Teamwork,' I agree, and Abe grins widely.

'It's Stan's turn next week, right?' Melody

A capable person is able to do things well.

checks. 'We could talk to Edie, too. And apparently Denny toured the world! The residents here are really cool. Why didn't you tell me?'

'I sort of tried,' I say with a smile.

'I'll just have a quick chat with Stan. Research, y'know.'

Abe turns to me. 'She's really good at the presenting thing, isn't she?' he says. We fold up my dad's old tripod. 'You have an actual stepsister! Well, almost ... When's the wedding again?'

'Two weeks from today,' Mum trills, gliding up behind us. 'A registry office do. Nice and simple.' Melody's a bit disappointed she can't wear a dress that looks like a meringue and put the whole thing on her channel, but Stefano's being very strict now. No flouncy dress. No channel. 'Just a few nice photos to remember the day.'

'And a big party afterwards, with everyone invited,' I tell Abe.

'Your mum's arranged for us to use the Beach Cafe after hours,' I continue. 'It'll be epic!'

Mum bustles off to make tea for the residents. Abe and I watch Melody. She chats to Stan, Edie and Denny, pausing to jot down notes. 'I guess she's not so bad,' Abe says. 'At least, not when she drops the superstar act. Maybe she can help us add in the titles and graphics on the documentary? D'you think she'd be into that?'

'She'd love it,' I tell him. 'She likes hot chocolate, too. And some of those old sci-fi re-runs on TV. I haven't seen her dunk biscuits, but we could get her to try!'

'Looks like we might need another armchair for the den then,' Abe says.

Chapter 8

Melody gets a new dress for the wedding, but it's bright blue and not flouncy. She wears it with stripy tights and blue trainers. I get new trainers too, which I wear with my favourite jeans and a stripy top. Mum goes all vintage in a blue fluffy cape and a cream dress. She borrowed it from Marie, who wore it to get married in 1972.

'Something old, something new, something borrowed, something blue,' Mum says. She is referring to an old rhyme that is supposed to bring brides good luck. 'The dress is old and borrowed. The shoes are new. The cape is blue. We're ready!'

Mum's care home friends crowd into the registry office, with Abe and Carole, and Stefano's mates.

When the registrar pronounces them married, Mum and Stefano look so starry-eyed that I just feel happy for them.

To refer to someone or something is to mention them or speak about them.

Mum throws her small bunch of flowers into the crowd. Everyone laughs because Edie catches it. Apparently, that means that she'll be next to get married.

'I'm 87!' she shrieks, cackling.

Mum wants to go along the pier before the party. 'Dino, will you take some photos of us?'

So Mum, Stefano and I stride along the seafront, past the cafe. Carole, Abe and a bunch of other friends are hanging 'Just Married' banners across the windows.

We walk to the end of the pier. Mum and Stefano pose together. The sea and sky are streaked with red and gold. I've only taken a couple of shots when Melody bounds up. She has four ice cream cones with sprinkles.

I switch my phone to the selfie setting and take several of the four of us bunched up together, a new family, laughing and eating ice cream at the end of the pier.

'Right, party time!' Stefano cheers, but I hesitate. I'm not quite ready to leave.

I hang back and ask Mum if I can quickly call Dad.

'Of course, Dino,' she says. 'Just five minutes, though, and then join us. I can't celebrate without my best boy!'

They walk slowly back, and I pick out the best ice cream shots. I click on three, sending them to Dad with the message 'Talk now?' My phone rings a moment later.

'Dino, fab photos!' Dad says. 'How did it go?'

'It was good,' I tell him. 'I've never been to a wedding before. And they're happy, Mum and Stefano. That's what matters, right?'

'Definitely,' he says. 'Families change and that's difficult. You know I'll always love you no matter what. But I'm glad your mum is happy again. Looks like you've got yourself a new family, Dino. And you're right at the centre of it!'

Right at the centre of it. The idea of it fills

me up with a weird, fizzy happiness that feels like it could bubble over. I look out beyond the end of the pier, across the sea. The setting sun has tipped the waves with gold.

'Dad?' I say. 'Remember when you used to tell me that if you stand at the end of the pier and look hard enough, you can see forever?'

He laughs. 'Sounds like the kind of thing I'd say!'

'Well, it's just ... I think I know what you mean now.'

Dad laughs, and I turn the phone to show him the setting sun behind me. I wave goodbye to my dad. Then I hang up and run along the pier towards the cafe.

There's a party in full swing there and I want to be right in the middle of it.